Who's That Banging on the Ceiling?

by Colin McNaughton

CANDLEWICK PRESS
CAMBRIDGE, MASSACHUSETTS

For Françoise, Ben, and Tim

First U.S. paperback edition 1994
First published in Great Britain in 1992 by Walker Books Ltd., London.

Library of Congress Cataloging-in-Publication Data

McNaughton, Colin.
Who's that banging on the ceiling? : a multistory story / by
Colin McNaughton. —1st U.S. ed.
Summary: People on each floor of an apartment building try to
guess what is making the noise they hear coming from above.
ISBN 1-56402-105-X (hardcover)—ISBN 1-56402-384-2 (paperback)
[1. Apartment houses—Fiction. 2. Noise—Fiction.
3. Imagination—Fiction.]   I. Title.
PZ7. M23256Wh   1992
[E]—dc20   91-58768

2 4 6 8 10 9 7 5 3 1

Printed in Hong Kong

The pictures in this book were done in watercolor and ink.

Candlewick Press
2067 Massachusetts Avenue
Cambridge, Massachusetts 02140

Home Sweet Home!

"What's that clack, clack, clacking
on the ceiling?" says Mrs. Manky
on the ground floor…

"It sounds like a dinosaur dancing the fandango!"

But that would be silly!
"What's that boing, boing, boinging?"
says Mrs. Fettle on the first floor…

"It sounds like elephants on pogo sticks!"

But that would be silly!
"What's that splish, splosh, splashing?"
says Mrs. Dutz on the second floor…

"It sounds like a sea battle!"

But that would be silly!
"What's that grunt, snort, slobbering?"
says Mrs. Gowk on the third floor…

"It sounds like a pigsty!"

But that would be silly!
"What's that squeak, squeak, squeaking?"
says Mr. Clarts on the fourth floor...

"It sounds like giant mice!"

But that would be silly!
"What's that crash, boom, twanging?"
says Mrs. Tarly-Toot on the fifth floor…

"It sounds like a rock and roll show!"

But that would be silly!
"What's that moo, cluck, quacking?"
says Mr. Plodge on the sixth floor...

"It sounds like a farmyard!"

But that would be silly!
"What's that ow! ouch! yowing?"
says Mrs. Haddaway on the seventh floor…

"It sounds like a fight!"

But that would be silly!
"What's that argh-ee-argh-ee-arghing?"
says Mr. Chebble on the eighth floor…

"It sounds like Tarzan of the Apes!"

But that would be silly!
"What's that huff, puff, puffing?"
says Mrs. Gadgee on the ninth floor…

"It sounds like the big bad wolf!"

But that would be silly!
"What's that zap, bleep, blooping?"
says Mr. Dunch on the tenth floor...

"It sounds
like King Kong
tap dancing!"

The End!

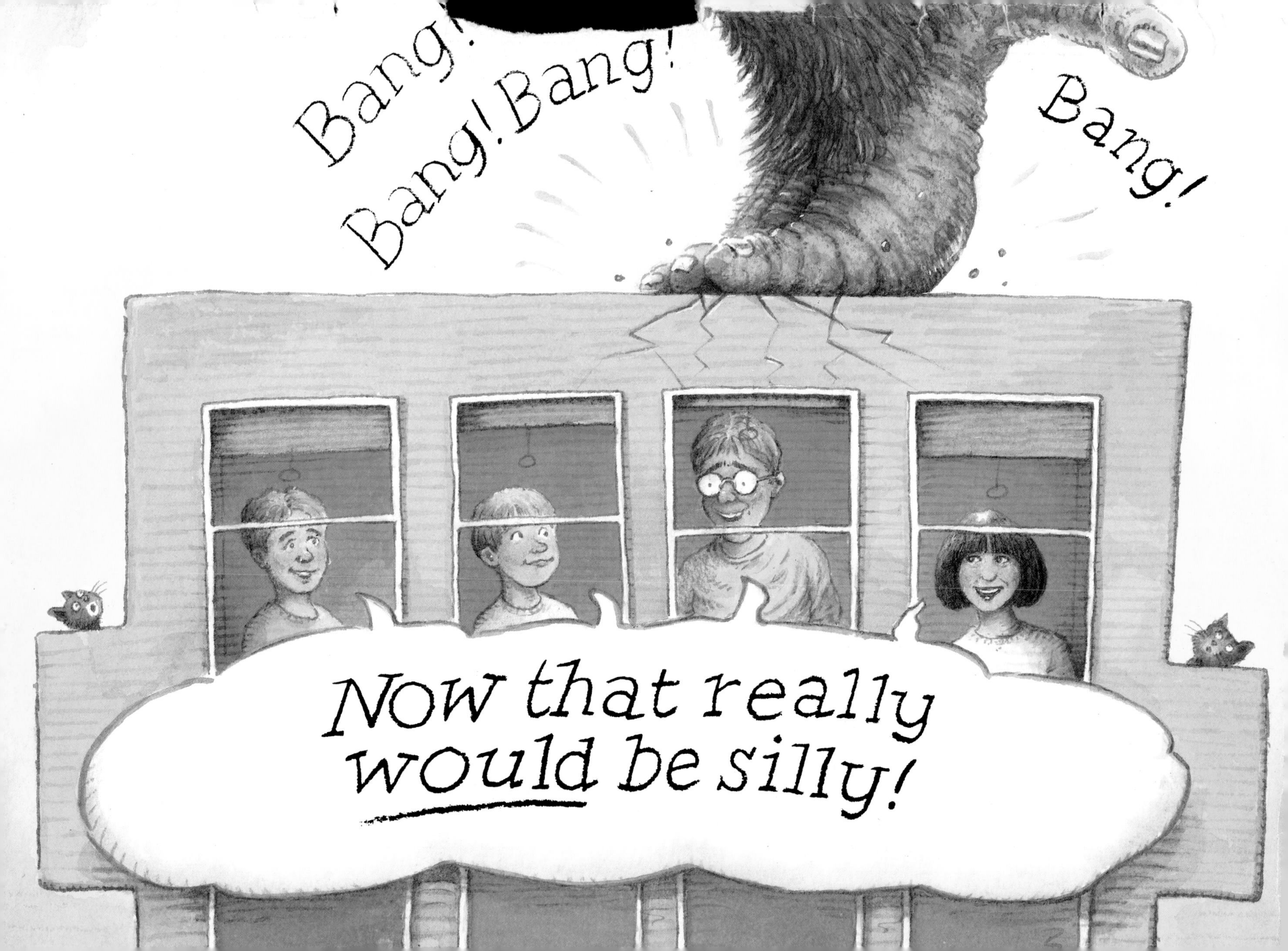
Bang!
Bang! Bang!
Bang!
Now that really would be silly!

But that would be silly!
"Who's that banging on the ceiling?"
says Mrs. Hacky-Mucky on the top floor…

"It sounds like an alien invasion!"